Beau

Is Non-Binary of Everything

Ladys

Translation by Monique A. Jira

Beau is Non-Binary of Everything

Author: Ladys
Translation: Monique A. Jira
Cover Artist: W. Neith
Proofreader: April Cummings

Ladys

Bangkok, Thailand.

Ordering Information:

For details, contact thatfrogpublishing@gmail.com

Book ISBN: 978-1-915214-66-9

thatfrogbooks.com

For

Your Bella Beau

Dedicated to the pursuing embrace
in the day I surrendered.

"

The angel has black wings,
likes an orange cat,
and purple Tutti Fruttis.

"

Table of Contents

Prologue

"Hello. Are you an angel?"

Since the first time we met, the *tiny human* called me that. Not being exceptional, all tiny humans have called me that.

"My father told me that if I am a good boy, an angel will grant me a wish. Is it true?"

These tiny humans understand my language. Their minds produce vast philosophies, way beyond any boundary or limits of their petite body—alas, the same minds wane and find only limits once they have grown up.

My physique that they see is what they desire to see...

"You are a girl just like me."

"You are a man, like my dad."

Man. Woman. Humans revere creating definitions to categorize things. But in every occasion, every period, and every epoch—some humans break away the categories and emerge past the descriptions of segregation.

"You are so pretty. I want to be just like you."

Humans build fences and frames that are too narrow for their own groups. In reality, these frames are pointless. I have always thought so.

“You are a girl. Girls are weak. I won’t play with you.”

"You are a man; I can't play with you."

And some tiny humans do not understand my language. Or for some of those who do, they are afraid.

“You have black wings. Black is a scary color.”

"Are you an angel of death? You will kill my family and me!?"

“Mom! There is a ghost!”

At last, they could not sense my existence.

Black...

Humans seem to despise and fear this color. The color that I recognize is the night when the Moon and all the stars vanish. For these humans, I am not an angel for the color of my wings.

But that one day, the day I found a peaceful solace in a small garden on Jeju Island. While my body rested on the soft grass, my eyes eased on the blue sky. I shifted my gaze to a peach on a peach tree and imagined its taste. That day, I met a tiny human named Kwon Cho.

“Miss Angel...you are so beautiful.”

I have heard the word *beautiful* for the entirety of my existence—unsure of its characteristics other than the form and flesh humans desire to see.

“I like your wings.”

Tiny human, do you like the color black?

“No, I like pink.”

The tiny human's small face, the face I could not see clearly, bowed down and stared at her tiny hands. Finally, she mumbled softly, quietly, but I understood.

"Actually, I like blue, but a girl should like pink."

Why...

"Everyone said so."

No...not true at all. Choose again. Choose the color you like. This concept of the distinction between man and woman is already ludicrous. Don't impose limits like those grownup humans.

"If you said that, then I like blue and purple, and I think orange is also nice. Actually, I also like pink if it is yogurt. Green is also a yummy one if it is a Tutti Frutti."

Hmm...I am more relieved.

"And black. Because your wings are black, I like your wings."

It crossed my mind that I let out a smile for the tiny human.

"What is your name, Miss Angel?"

My name? Humans such as you cannot pronounce my name. Name me. Anything.

"Omma[1] said *Cho* means beautiful. You should be named the same. Because you are beautiful."

My name and yours are the same? I asked. The tiny

---

[1] Omma (엄마) is Korean means Mother.

human shook her head and wrinkled her nose.

"Pick other words...this is too confusing."

Then what name should one choose? Humans are too complex; their languages are too diverse.

Bellus, Beauty, Bella, Beau...I recited in each human language I knew. The tiny human cried out excitedly.

"Bella Beau...your name is Bella Beau!"

If you wish, Bella Beau then.

****

"Here...I drew you."

Do you mean this figure like a scarecrow in an empty field but with pointy wings? Intriguing. I like art made by humans. I am amazed and bewildered. Despite having such a short time to live, a human can produce inventions, mirrored creations that existed before my existence. This, I always admired.

Throughout the summer, as short as the instance the Sun sank and disappeared into the sea—I had become a friend of Kwon Cho and a cat named Tin Tin.

She drew an impression of me and filled all the spaces within the leather-covered notebook. Her gifts in exchange were some purple Tutti Fruttis—the only color she disliked—because of its distinct smell and piercing taste. My senses were not born to perceive such sensations, and I perhaps can call it *delicious*, only perhaps.

Kwon Cho used that word.

****

When the summer ended and this rejuvenation period came to an end, before departing, I erased memories of me from the tiny human, just like always—touching my thumbs on both of her tiny eyelids, then all the recollections my shape and form recalled as beautiful, magnificent, and flawless shall be gone, just like fading smoke.

I spread my wings, took off, and flew invisibly across the sky at dawn. The taste of the Tutti Fruttis still lingered. A flicker of hope quietly emerged within the emptiness of my chest.

I hope that the next time we meet, Kwon Cho still sees and understands the language of Bella Beau. That is my wish.

****

"Your wings...so beautiful."

Summertime returned. It was a celebratory moment. My wish was answered.

"My name is Kwon Cho. What is your name?"

Bella Beau...

Chapter 1

That Angel Face

Bella Beau... Beautiful and beautiful—the person's name and last name of this meaning. Coupled with the exquisite appearance beyond words, for Kwon Cho, everything exceeded the realm of reality. In a small café that overlooked the view of the Ponte Vecchio, the medieval bridge gradually lit up, and the illuminating amber hues reflected in the dark blue water. The person on the other side of the table scooped up and nibbled her Tutti Frutti gelato. Kwon Cho was startled by choice of the place chosen. Collectors that won auctions of her art pieces, if they want more discussions, usually request a place for dinner—chewing food and sipping wine while dialogues of art ensue for hours. But this time, the empty gelato paper cup and small ice cream spoon laid silently in front of the auction winner for the perfectly complete but unfinished stone sculpture. The sculpture that its artist and creator bestowed the name

'An Angel and the Black Wings.'

In truth, the marble was white and the face of the Angel mysterious—it was empty. The only sound explanation left was the beauty described cannot be defined by any chisel or hammer.

Kwon Cho chewed sticky jellies that once hid inside sweet yogurt gelato. She stared at Bella Beau, who barely spoke a word. It was her who asked the woman questions. Trades—Bella Beau said she was an expert. And hundreds of art pieces from world-renowned artists in her private gallery were obtained through such means. She mentioned it as if she had personally handled the deals herself. With them, the artists who had lived hundreds of years before. This sounded incredible beyond truth, like her name, like her flawless face.

Kwon Cho's dark eyes stared at the design on the midnight black suit worn over a dark purple vest. In the shape of magnolia, the embroidery reminded her of the hidden tattoo on her arm, covered by a white shirt and light brown coat. For some unexplained reason, Kwon Cho adored magnolia. She drew magnolia flowers and had a magnolia tattoo. When a pigeon flew past an open window nearby, a strange flickering feeling arose suddenly without reason. Her hand with a black-wing tattoo on the knuckle raised to her chest. Her heart was pounding loudly; it was thumping as she shifted her gaze to meet those pair of obsidian eyes.

Bella Beau raised her eyebrows. Her jaw moved as she chewed and tasted sweet and sour jellies. The hanging bell on the door jingled. She let out a soft smile before asking. Her voice was soothingly low.

"Kwon Cho...does your angel have black wings?"

The sky shown through the window was turning dark. The smell of rain and earth became poignant. The one who was asked nodded before answering softly, "I believe so."

Black...yes, angels may have white wings. Or any color. Or no wings at all. But if the angel in question is the faceless statue—it has "midnight black wings, spreading out to the sky." And she had absolute confidence that the angel was beautiful...so beautiful. This sounded shallow and superficial, but her intention was to the contrary. For Kwon Cho, the beauty she felt is not the divinity of churches and temples, not the shapes one can touch or see; for Kwon Cho, beauty lays deep...

It may be the beauty that describes a singular art. Or the grandeur of Rafael's Philosophers in a grand hall. The white in the rays of light and black in the ominous shadow of Caravaggio's art. Or the cerulean blue sky brushed with briefness of moments by Monet. The beauty breeds confidence in artists and encourages them to create. The beauty offers a comforting embrace when the world turns into the color of paint wash-water or the green on bitter pills in opaque bottles. The beauty is profound and cosmic enough to compare to bits of description for the black-wings angel's existence.

"It's almost raining. Kwon Cho, do you like the rain?"

Let's go for a walk. A rather strange invitation. Should one not walk along the rivers and bridges on a day with a clear sky instead? No matter what feelings Florence on a somber day elicited, Kwon Cho nodded in agreement **because she liked rainy days all the same.**

****

Five years ago

If the sky is clear, if she kept an open mind and kept on staring, she may, at last, see an angel.

Thump thump thump

The sound of a hammer's full force on the end of a chisel echoed all over Kwon Cho's high-ceiling studio just like always. Bits of marble, large and small, fell to the concrete floor. The artist touched the sharp nose of the sculpture for an inspection. She had to wear protective safety goggles and a mask to shield her from white dust that flew all over. Kwon Cho, in a dim colored jumpsuit, disliked electrical equipment. She disliked the sound of an electric drill and other equipment that was designed for efficiency and reduced the total time of production—when she had to pay attention to the details, this equipment rushes the process; too fast, too bothersome, and sway her attention like an iron pendulum in a grand old grandfather clock. It may take some time to have a sculpture made in this studio, but the outcome is an exquisite beauty worth waiting for.

The tip of a small chisel pierced bit by bit into the marble, a long scrape formed a line, leaving consistent loud noises disturbing the usual quiet room otherwise filled with the sounds of the artist's breathing and her own thoughts. What seemed like an eternity lasted until her strand of attention worn out. Kwon Cho knit her brows. She dropped the heavy hammer on the worktable, then the mask and goggles followed. She washed her hands in the basin, wiped them off hastily with her trousers, and picked up a small opaque bottle next to a sketchbook.

She sighed heavily and angrily when she realized that there was only one green pill left. Her hand, scarred and recently healed, lifted up the small bottle to her mouth. She swallowed the pill just then. She brought herself to stand in front of an open window, looked out into Mr. Ricardo's vegetable garden, took out a cigarette from its carton, lighted it up with a lighter, breathed in, and breathed out while contemplating on the floating and fading smoke.

Her emotions had colors more similar to the smoke than the colors of the sky.

Today's weather is a delight. The day an apricot tree started to bloom. Soon there might be yellow spots brushed all over the green leaves. The view might look more refreshing, the sky bluer. Blue and yellow always embrace each other well. Her thoughts circulated back to the sculpture and the face of Athena for a long while. Her slim fingers that held the cigarette motioned down and crushed the cigarette into a fractured coffee saucer. Kwon Chow planned to keep the saucer until it shattered into pieces—which will not take long.

The young woman took a deep sigh, raised her arms to stretch, gazed out to see a small flower for one last time before turning her eyes back to the cement wall...

Black wings were the first things that Kwon Cho saw.

Her arm froze midair and gradually dropped. A complete shock was shown as her eyes widened. She gasped. And although she uttered no words, in her head, she screamed.

An angel stood in the middle of the studio. Black wings spread wide. The angel looked slightly bemused while admiring the marble sculpture.

"An a-angel?"

Yes, you can call me that. But I have a name.

My name...is Bella Beau.

With the language of an angel, the bewildered human humbly understood.

It is as if today...the sky is bright enough. The verses mentioned by the angel were parallel to timeless gospel hymns at the church. The sound of heated wind in the summer. And once paused, the deafening silence echoed like the hall where Rondanini Pietà stood still.

Is an angel this magnificently beautiful?—a question and an exclamation that was declared clearly evidence in the eyes of this vulnerable human.

Of all the sculptures in the room, none could be compared to the black-winged angel. Those feathers were radiant under sunlight. Even one black feather was unrivaled by all arts. Her impassive expression betrayed her genuine emotion—the ambitious hunger for art boiled inside Kwon Cho. If this was a dream, she wished for more clarity when awake. But if it was not...

"Bella Beau..." Because she did not think of the reason for the angel's arrival—what did they want or why did they appear? No assumptions seemed ordinary but let it be. She swallowed and approached Bella Beau slowly while not taking her eyes off the angel.

"I want to create...a sculpture with you as a model."

Flawless, every inch under the scrutiny of her eyes, she saw only an absolute exquisiteness and perfection.

How can an angel be this impeccable?

****

"I want to draw you, Beau."

The second time we met, the tiny human and her tiny face uttered the same plea. The request I never deny. This time Kwon Cho created a replica of me with a watercolor.

She soaked and tore the paper on the first attempt. Try again. I said. She still used too much water on the second and third attempts. Above the ranch, the Sun began to set. My replica was completed on the fourth try.

On the drying paper, my hair was red like Tin Tin. Short-haired and with a beret on like a British artist. The black wings and cloak were dotted from water drops. Kwon Chow gave me this art piece. And Frutti Tuttis. I chose the purple one.

"You like purple ones? You know, they are not really a grape flavor."

Is that so? What a shame. I have not known what grapes taste like for humans.

"The flavor is cranberry."

The same goes for cranberry. Then, I will remember that cranberry tastes like purple Tutti Fruttis.

The next day. And the next day. And the next day. I sat, laid down, flew unhurriedly, and fluttered my wings lightly above ground. All for this tiny human seated on the soft grass, drawing a replica of me. Watercolor tubes and pan scattered around her like small flowers blooming between the grass.

"Are you tired, Beau?"

Tired? No. Your hour may be a mere instance in my world.

I answered, flying midair. I moved my wings slightly to shield away the afternoon sun, so the tiny human could continue to draw under my shadow.

****

The inception of a new project occupied the days and nights within Kwon Cho's studio. Time seemed to stand still and all but similar. Only noises were the sound of the footsteps from her sneakers walking back and forth between the model, a sketchbook, and a figure built from clay. But when the clay started to take shape, the artist shook her head— tired and discontent; she turned away from the grey clay figure.

She put down her hands, hurriedly searched for those green pills before taking one in. She drank all the black coffee in one gulp. Her paint-stained hands massaged her furrowed brows, leaving a trace.

All meanwhile, an angel standing on a wooden stand looked on and said nothing. The situation kept repeating itself; the human stared into that exquisite face, measured and noted down numbers, worked on the clay, voiced out disapprovals, walked out, lit a cigarette, and gazed absent-mindedly before she was back into staring at the faultless face again.

"Bella Beau"

Yes?

"It seems that...your exquisite face is at odds with this clay." That was all she said before walking close to the model whose black wings wavered lightly, whiffling a bit of wind that gave a scent of old book papers mixed with vanilla candles.

Kwon Cho took out a small paintbrush from her shirt pocket, touched the tip of it to her tight lips. She squinted and knit her brows while remembering details of the nape and collarbone. She mumbled and went on to mess with the clay.

Bella Beau's black eyes observed the old paintbrush and how its wooden end was pushed into the clay sculpture, leaving a dent representing a dent of a collarbone, then the brush was back into the shirt pocket.

****

"Do angels have magic?"

Maybe, sometimes. I answered. The magic the human mentioned has more conditions than simply a yes or no. But this time, I did not speak of it. The tiny human marched in front of me, laughed loudly, and chased after a butterfly into a vegetable garden. She called those green plant bulbs lettuces.

"It is almost my birthday. Will you give me a gift?"

I stood motionless and contemplated. Then we walked to the end of the lettuce garden, and I answered *Yes, I have a gift for you, Kwon Cho.*

If she was grown, such a gift might be worthless and laughable, but Kwon Cho was a tiny human. So when I picked up her paintbrush from the ground, murmured meaningless words of the hymn from my world, scooped up fallen dried flowers from the floor, sprinkled them all over the small paintbrush, and handed it to her. She screamed with joy and called that ordinary paintbrush ***a magical paintbrush***...

A magical paintbrush...when Kwon Cho believed, I also saw that it was truly magical. Of course, no magic was from me, and neither from meaningless hymns nor dried flowers.

The magic materialized...because of her.

Chapter 2

Angel in the Rain

The rain was about to pour. Kwon Cho wrinkled her nose, placed her hands on her hips, cocked her head while contemplating on the drying clay figure. The knotted brows were apparent on her tired face. *Not at all. Not even close.* She sighed and wiped the dried clay off her hands with an old cloth. She walked to close a large window that shielded the studio from the wind that often comes with humidity and the musky smell of rain and earth. When she turned, the angel had disappeared from the wooden stand in the middle of the studio. Instead, the black-winged figure examined the clay sculpture created in Angel's own image. And when the two stood side by side, the art creator was certain that the clay sculpture she dedicated days creating was utterly different from the original. The proportion and measurements may be close, and one could even say perfect for the stage of building a clay replica prior to working on marble.

But when she looked upon it, Kwon Cho could only shake her head with shame. Her small hand searched for a cigarette inside her jumpsuit. But once retrieved, she could only stand still and crossed her arms because she had just realized that the window was closed.

Do you have Tutti Frutti, Kwon Cho?

The young lady raised her eyebrows. The obsessive thought in finding the difference between the original model and the replica vanished and was replaced by astonishment. *The angel likes Tutti Frutti?*

"I don't have one." She answered and remembered that in the past, she used to always have it in her pocket. But the sweet taste and the smell of artificial fruits could no longer whisk away any distress. Now she only had a pack of cigarettes and a small bottle of green pills.

So unfortunate. The angel whispered softly. Kwon Cho crossed her arms and suddenly realized that she also missed that snack, the fruit flavor snack, but not the purple ones. She did not like the purple Tutti Fruttis at all—they reminded her of liquid medicine her granny forced her to take when she was a kid. But here, Kwon Cho found a strangeness in her likes and dislikes—despite her disapproval, the young lady sensed that the tiny purple Tutti Fruttis had something special—they are not leftover pieces in the bottom of the box, someone like those purple pieces. Green is special. Red is special. Yellow is special...

"What color do you like? I mean for Tutti Frutti."

Purple...I like purple.

The angel answered. And the human smiled softly. *That is it. The purple ones are also special* because the angel liked purple Tutti Fruttis.

****

The human sight could see everything clearly during days with a clear sky but dim down under the cloudy atmosphere. Hence, I could walk among them without the worry of my black wings being seen because that may potentially lead to troubles—some humans might scream, some cars might crash, and that child over there might throw his soft cream at me.

"Beau, you have never gotten wet by the rain?"

Rain exists in my world. And I could get wet by the rain.

Kwon Cho continued to ask about my world, but I could hardly answer. To compare things between that world and this one can hardly be done. *Because in my world, we have no measurement, no identification, and no categorization.* So, it was challenging to force those concepts into the casts created by humans.

When we met again, Kwon Cho was a slightly grown human. *Middle School.* She said she was in that class. And the clothes she wore were the same as other teenagers, soaked in the rain, walking on the same footpath as us. Trees with pink blossoms bloomed along both sides of the street. In this weather, Kwon Cho pulled out her light-colored cardigan to wear on top of her white shirt. My black wings shielded her from the raindrops. She confessed to liking the rain, but since it can ruin the sketchbook that she always carried around, she disliked it in this regard.

"Your wings are remarkable." This was another time Kwon Cho praised my wings. On the first time, she complimented them for their color—being a shade of black darker than the color of her mother's eyes. Another time, she admired their shape as being like birds in a mystical tale unbeknownst to me. This time, she appreciated them for their vastness. For my appearance, this time, as I investigated my own reflection, I may be called *a boy*. My hair was brown in the color of tree bark, freckles on my cheeks, and a foot taller than Kwon Cho. When she complimented on those attributes, I enjoyed no joy because, as certain as the Sun, everything changed each time we met. *But when it was my wings she admired*, I embraced such joy with a smile, such joyous dance inside my chest, and her words marked the moment I admired my wings the most—more than ever, it might even be the most since the genesis of my own existence.

****

Those angel wings are so remarkable—this thought emerged in Kwon Cho's mind while she was walking slowly under the black wings that shielded her from the rain and strong wind. Sneakers and leather shoes—the two walked through the uneven pavement, passed all familiar yellow and brown buildings and houses. Both a small pack of cigarettes and a Tutti Frutti box were in Kwon Cho's hand. She just bought them from a convenience store two blocks away from the studio. And because her stomach growled, Kwon Cho slowed down her steps and told Bella Beau (whom she was sure had no need for the same kind of food) that she needed something to eat because there was nothing left in the fridge. They ended up going into a pizza bistro that appeared more like a home than a restaurant.

The two sat across from each other. The young artist asked the black-winged angel who was eating sweet snacks, "Why couldn't anyone see you?"

Perhaps, people can. But in this weather, they could not. The angel often talked about the weather. Kwon Cho was told that humans could see angels on days with the bright and clear sky, and **they must have a firm belief of an angels' existence to see them**. That was all Beau answered before sitting in silence like a statue. Kwon Cho picked up a piece of Parma ham pizza. While she was chewing, a thought emerged—*Me? I believe that angels exist? Maybe it is so.* Because if anyone was to deny their existence, she would argue that for humans, how cosmic and meticulous our eyesight can be?

"Bella Beau, when you looked at that clay sculpture,

do you think it looks like you?" She asked because she thought that perhaps an angel's sight might be superior to humans'—seeing the differences she did not expect. Those differences distinguished the shape and form of that sculpture completely from this angel sitting in front of her.

Once asked, Bella Beau thought of the replica in an angel's image, built from clay and shaped by the sharp-end of the paintbrush and a stainless-steel sculpting tool—it was sculpted and molded by hands of the artist who called this angelic form as perfect exquisite beauty. The more the angel contemplated the similarities, the more exactness the art was executed—that shape and form shared the resemblance to the angel's feminine features as reflected on the glass of red wine on the table. Once looking into a large mirror in the restaurant's corner, the reflection of a lady dressed in black looked back—all the exact same as the sculpture. If there should be a difference, then it was the thoughts wandering in her cognition—the only gift that the clay sculpture lacked.

Kwon Cho. When spoken, the angel found another difference—words. The sculpture's silence is an expected norm. **If you do not want to create me from my replica, why did you not build any creation from my essence?**

****

Kwon Cho painted her toenails in the color of Hydrangea

Blue. She hummed a song that sounded like the wind, and meanwhile, I looked down at my own nails, for they were painted with the same nail polish. When she hesitated whether to get me involved, I fully understood her intention.

Once, I was a friend of Charlie, a tiny human everyone called 'a boy.' Charlie liked to paint his body with colors and glitters that seemed almost magical. I myself saw the whole ordeal as magnificent and creative. But then one day, he ran to me crying, big ugly bruises on his stomach and right eye. I handed him a light pink lipstick, such painting tool that usually brought a bright smile to Charlie's little face. But that one time, he pushed it away—he shoved me and violently shouted words—and soon after, he could no longer perceive my existence. Kwon Cho might fear for me as I may have bruises on this boyish body of mine, just like Charlie.

Not to worry...angels can have their nails in any color. Once she heard, she smiled wide and took my hands to begin painting. My nails, she said in glee, were a lot larger than her own. And with such reason, she proceeded to draw a white flower on my thumbnail.

A magnolia. I remember the name of that flower well.

****

The sound of a charcoal pencil slowly scraping on the surface of a large marble. The enormous chunk was several feet taller than the artist, and its weight was heavy enough to break the cement floor if handled carelessly. After crudely cutting off unnecessary parts—determined, her eyes turned back and forth between the model and her own sketch. Instead of its usual place on the stand, the clay sculpture was relocated to the back of the studio—in this process, it was no longer necessary.

Hours had passed—or for humans, a unit of weeks was more applicable. Kwon Cho worked with a measurement made of several wooden rulers and sticks—placing it on the thigh and moving it to the angel's toes. Her fingertips gently felt the shallowness and strength of the physique to remember its depth. At times, she noted down numbers. And every time she looked up, Kwon Cho always found herself staring into those obsidian eyes. All she could do was forcing a chuckle and shake her head.

"Does an angel always make one feel this way?"

This way? What kind then...

"An admiration, an infatuation, I think."

Such effects are to be expected from my face and flesh, for you see anything you desire to see.

"I don't know..."

"Perhaps, the feeling runs deeper, Bella Beau."

Chapter 3

Ballad of Angel

Once upon the first time we met, Kwon Cho's tiny knees—those knees that looked like knotholes on an apple tree branch, were scratched. She stumbled on the rocky ground near the marshy pond. She then turned and looked at me, trying to hold back her tears, but then her lips quivered, and she let out a loud cry. That one time, I understood that the source of anguish for the tiny human came from physical wounds—the bruises or the dripping of blood. *But this time, I could not find abrasions, bruises, or blood on her skin.*

Kwon Cho's sketchbook was overlaid with papers that I had never seen before. "I am really not good at math." She murmured tiredly, laid down on the bed, and sighed. As if the document called **'High School Transcript'** was a rock-strewn road whose roughness caused her knees to bruise. "Actually, Physics, for me, is also an abomination. I'm not good at Chemistry either. It seems like I'm not good at anything." Do humans judge their talents based on a few letters? I was just aware of this fact, surprisingly. Those letters were simply...letters. Only five of them and a list of ten subjects. How can it be enough to justify their merits when humans are as countless as the stars and as diverse as the earth's flora? I do not understand this absurdity at all.

Kwon Cho reached out her arms, and I bowed low—for her fingers could touch the feathers on my wings. Such a delight, she seemed. A reminder emerged of the day she laid leisurely on the yellow grass and casually stretched out her hands to caress the surrounding tall grass. *But then she cried.* Kwon Cho cried. Her tears flowed; her body trembled. Invisible and mysterious those wounds were—and I stood helpless in healing her. *In the dark abyss inside her soul where those wounds lived, and I could only watch.*

****

After circling around the marble for several days and nights, the morning came that Kwon Cho broke her eyes from the sculpture. The silence absorbed all striking sounds of hammer and chisel. Gone was the white dust floating in the sunlight. The light rays shone through the round windows resembling stained glass mosaic in the Church of Christ. The tall glass panes stretched to the ceiling—they were made in the shape of a white flower, not the immortalization of powerful or sacred man. Kwon Cho poured coffee into her cup, tossed out the cigarette butts and ashes, then walked unhurriedly, sipping the light bitter taste before reaching the canvas that had just been draped over a wooden frame last night. "That is for rent." She talked to Bella Beau, who stood behind her. The artist picked a piece of charcoal to sketch as commissioned, "but with this price I charge, I could probably also buy a few tubes of quality oil paints." The winged figure nodded, stepped closer, those wings widened slightly, and the angel's puzzled face looked down at the opaque bottle falling from the oversized jeans' pocket. "And these meds for the whole of next month." Kwon Cho turned around and smiled at the angel. She picked up and kept the small bottle in her pocket. Then all her attention was turned to the art that stained her palm.

Those pills must be tastier than green Tutti Frutti pieces. In silence, Bella Beau assumed humans must have parallel thoughts once they have grown. For Kwon Cho had let the sweets gone emptied without further need of refilling—her decision on those green pills were, however, diverted—never had she let them go absent for long. *Delightfully delectable pills they must be*.

****

Tin Tin breathed out a sound of stone-scrapping on a tree

bark. Kwon Cho let out a breathing sound I could find no comparison for. I carried the orange-fur creature in my arms. I tilted my head to snuggle against his softness and warmth. *Tin Tin only sleeps all day.* Kwon Cho said. But that was not entirely true. For when she was in a slumber, I ventured out into the world with him. Tin Tin ran through the vegetable gardens, meadows, and the roof of the shed—how alert and active he was.

Humans are strange creatures. They live as if preparing a coffin for tomorrow is a complete necessity. A cat like me will surely die before them. In a few years, or maybe not even a year. But I still run on the field when I want to run. If humans want to run on the field, they will find only limitations—as if they go for a run, they will not prepare the coffin in time—How about the painted wood and hammered nails? And the flowers surrounding the casket, will they bloom in time? Well! No wonder they have only one life. If they have nine lives like me and have to prepare nine coffins, the thought of it is already tiresome, is it not?

That one night, we laid down on the grass field and looked at the moonlight together; Tin Tin relayed his message to me. And now he nudged me to look at Kwon Cho. She rested on her chin at the table, writing, swirling her wooden pencil with her fingertips and alternating in lightly tapping the table.

Hey, angel, tell her to stop building her own coffin. Well, at least rest for a while. Tin Tin said and walked away—

his furry self then rested in a box. His fluffy round shape looked like a loaf of fresh-milk bread Kwon Cho liked to eat for breakfast.

My eyes wandered out the window—the magnolias hadn't bloomed, but I begged them to.

And once she looked up from the table, Kwon Cho exclaimed in surprise—"Beautiful...since when did they bloom this much?" And she got up, picked up her drawing board and a bag full of paint tubes and brushes. "I am going outside to draw. Will you come with me, Bella Beau?"

Not bad, angel. Tin Tin said. And I could only smile. This time, Kwon Cho drew me standing in the midst of magnolias.

****

As the Sun disappeared from the stained-glass window, it was late afternoon when the artist lazily stretched out her arms, her hands stained with light brown paint. And when she turned to look behind, even with a sideways glance, the angel appeared to be observing the painting she was working on at the same site (and standing motionless in the same pose, if she was not mistaken). *Once more*, she questioned whether Bella Beau was, in truth, a sculpture.

She imagined Galatea—being created and cherished by Pygmalion. If the beauty was this paramount, doubtlessly the fall she took for this bottomless pit of infatuation, for the marble named Bella Beau, shall be severe. But then a reminder had its gentle nudge—no matter how persistent her endeavor, how accomplished her skills, the marble was incomparable to the beauty of the black-winged angel. And not to forget the poetic sweetness of those words. Let Pygmalion fancied Galatea's silence. Because, for Kwon Cho, even the angel's quiet whisper invited her to heed.

Kwon Cho soaked the paintbrush in oil. She slid the paint palate off the way and swept flat color tubes against the wall before leaning up and walking towards a vintage phonograph record player. The artist bent down, randomly choosing one record from a wooden box. Once the music blared out of the decades-old horn that was once glittering gold, she let the gravity take her as she sank herself on the sofa—stretching out her arms, taking off those thick, hot, uncomfortable trousers, massaging her aching neck, and eventually closed her eyes while listening to hit songs from the glorious '60s.

"Do angels have songs to listen to?"

Yes, definitely.

Her eyes closed, she could only hear a low voice replying—until a gentle breeze caressed her cheeks, her small nose smelled the floating scent of old books and vanilla. Kwon Cho opened her eyes to the black-winged angel standing within reach. She felt as if the Sun bid farewell upon the horizon and the twilight summoned—for the shadows cast from those large wings. "What kind of music is it? Is it like this song here?"

Not at all. One could compare it to the whistling sound of the wind, the flowing sound of rivers, the lively sound of leaves.

"Is it? Interesting."

And sometimes, those songs are similar to the sound of the Moon. Oh, actually, humans cannot hear any sound from the Moon.

"Um...if that's the case, I must really like it." Because the angel remained unmoving, Kwon Cho continued—"What you described are sounds that make me feel good, you know?"

It was unfortunate because those sounds mentioned were almost inaudible from this place. If the sounds of the city had not already overwhelmed, then it would be the restless noises inside her head that are never quieted enough for her to hear those angelic songs.

"Those songs must be precious...I am sure."

The angel remained silent. Those immaculate eyes glanced over a short sentence tattooed on Kwon Cho's thigh and shifted to another sentence close to an ankle.

The angel sings...

Not with my feet; it is my heart that dances.

****

To compare to the human realm, this time, for years, I had been watching Kwon Cho and her invisible wounds. Kwon Cho wept all too often, sometimes she broke down in sobs; at times, she cried out in silence. I had learned that grown humans might cry more often than tiny humans. Particularly, those muted cries without tears and any whimper—*Grown humans do that ceaselessly.* And at this time, on the overpass high up, hear the squealing sound of horns and the rustling uproar of passing steel engine cars below. My friend (who was not that grownup) was silently weeping. She walked to the edge of the overpass's fence, hung a navy-color coat, a part of her high school uniform, over the iron rod, and glared absently out into the deep orange sky.

We both stood in silence. Nonetheless, the surroundings were in turmoil, with a rushing commotion that completely drowned out the sound of the trees and the wind. Why did humans invent these sounds? How unpleasant they all were. In such wise, I paused in consideration for a moment before singing a song resonant to sounds of Spring. It was then that Kwon Cho's tired face suddenly smiled brightly before my eyes. In truth, her smile was a Spring I anticipated with hope to survive a harsh Winter.

Because the cold wind withered away flowers in my garden. And humans can wither just the same. I detest the thought. For I can build a glass house shielding flowers in the cold. But for humans, Kwon Cho said an embrace warms her heart, and music delights her days.

Warmth and delight—perhaps a Spring in the Human mind. Thus, my arms and wings embraced her, a woman in pain from invisible wounds. The songs of flowers, sunlight, and the wind was sung. I waited until her woundless smile returned to bid farewell with the touch of fingertips on both her eyelids.

****

The angel sat down beside Kwon Cho, who had fallen asleep. The vintage phonograph needle was lifted off the vinyl record that played till the end. The black-winged figure laid down on the concrete floor next to the sofa. In silence, Bella Beau stared at the ceiling higher up. The moonlight was tinted with colors from stained glass panes—it danced on the wooden surface. The breathing rhythm was a lullaby for the angel who had none. And meanwhile, the melody of a dark pine forest and high mountain range was lulling the human who was drowning in gloomy colors like the city sky.

Chapter 4

With the (Angel's) Assent

"Beau, why could a paint drop stain your skin when a raindrop can't?" was Kwon Cho's question. She drew a small black line with the tip of a paintbrush on the nape of my neck, passing a contour of the muscle as I was turning sideways. That line helped her recognize these forms—deep dents and bevels to be chiseled into the marble surface. And at this time, the torso of the angel replica revealed a glimpse of delicate beauty. *Because I consent.* The exact answer applied for the query on raindrops. Without consent, no fraction of substance can feel and sense the existence of an angel. *Never shall I get wet from raindrops. Never shall I sense the heat of a fire. Never shall I feel the chill of the wind. Nor will I disconcert with the taste of wine.* Even a Tutti Frutti that Kwon Cho thought was the angel's favorite, if without permission— the sweet and sour taste and the smell of cranberry as told by human—could never once materialize in the cognizance of the Master of One's Fate. "Consent?"

Yes…consent.

Another black line was drawn close by, "It's good that you can choose." *That's true…but not for everything.* The angel said with a mysterious smile. Actually, every story about Bella Beau was mysterious. Who else knows about angels (that are real angels)? Scientist? Kwon Cho once questioned and answered herself, but then she shook her head. *The wisdom that is (claimed) to be true, verifiable, and always being proved. Was it all?* She thought that was not the wisdom of the angel. The angelic body was not meant for them to be dissected. This beauty was not for anyone to weigh, measure, define or classify—nor should it be for archaeologists or historians to unearth the past to find a trace of truth. Conceding that Bella Beau had lived through the ages, those wings might have soared past the newly built pyramid, through the poetic rhythm from Homer's lips, through the collapse of the Temple of Athena, through the army of Napoleon—the man in flesh and blood beyond a mere painting of a hero on a white horse, through the artists who created the works that were auctioned off and set up in museums—through many things that students of history dream of seeing with their own eyes. A question was raised on the existence of any evidence for angels. Even the sight of this immaculate form was rare. Who else was bestowed the fortune of witnessing an angel? And one may find that *once believed, one could see*—an ostensibly universal truth but entirely personal that it can't be written down as a principle—for the reason of an open mind. This conclusion may contradict the evidence of science and beliefs or sometimes simply one's preferences. Kwon Cho recognized the struggle in the matter of being open-minded—virtually impossible even for her, on some agenda, to not succumb to accidental prejudice.

"If that is so, what can't you choose?" She stepped down from a ladder and placed the paintbrush in clean water, dyeing the invisible transparent liquid with swirling black paint. And then the angel answered. Below the marble dust-stained eyebrows, the artist's slanted eyes squinted with interest. "Anything that exudes from the human mind?"

Joy echoes a ringing bell. Sorrow is the whisking winds in the smell of mud. Pain has a piercing scream. Expectation whistles like the wind on the mountain top. Disappointment reverberates like a rock falling into the abyss. And countless others, both nameless and unnamed. All are too delicate for an angel's grate of consent to separate.

Yes, without you saying a word, I sense it all anyway.

"Then I can't even lie."

Perhaps. Because sadness can shout. But the saying "It's alright, I'm fine" is a mere whisper; even when shouting, it's still too soft. I heard it all in essence.

"*Hmm*...then I probably practically shouted at you." Kwon Cho sneered, sighed, and chuckled in a low voice that sounded like a swarm of bees. Her fingertip stroked the sharp iron chisel thoughtfully. She visually placed the projected outline on the soft white surface. "My shouts...are they really loud, Bella Beau?" To answer honestly, the angel would say that *sometimes*, the loudness drowned out the sound of a hammer. But because I saw no value in answering, my lips kept the silence and listened to the thumping sound of the hammer and chisel. While eyes staring at the fine white dust floating in the morning light, *Bella Beau loved the cloud of dust from the white marbles more than any cloud of smoke from a cigarette butt or Kwon Cho's mouth and nose.*

During the process of recreation, the artist, whose singular focus was on the art piece and the model, had more questions than usual. The same curiosity that appeared when she shifted her eyes and stumbled on small spots or corners of a painting. A corner where an unnamed person might once stand. If it was Artemisia's work, that person's face might be revealed only for a fraction, and the rest obscured with shadows. Though curious, Kwon Cho kept her mouth shut; she did not want to distract her own thoughts or interfere with the consistent thumping sound of a hammer. Besides, the angelic facial expressions and demeanor were extremely fitting. She thought to ask after finishing this section, but the moment passed and the chisel placed at another spot— until several hours had passed...

"Let's take a rest." Her shoulder and back ached, muscles convulsed in protest. Kwon Cho left her equipment on the table, picked a cigarette to hold between her lips. Her hands, bandaged around an index finger and middle finger, patted exploratively on the shirt and trouser pockets. She opened a wooden box and flipped over books to find a lighter forgotten elsewhere. "Do you see a lighter?" She could not find it even she when tried; asking the angel standing on the wooden pedestal in the middle of the room was a logical move. "Ugh, where is it?" She started to get upset when the answer was *I don't see any*. Her brows furrowed slightly while her lips, with a cigarette unlit, muttered complaints. As for Bella Beau—whose wings were fluttering and floating up from the ground—asked to look at a paper Kwon Cho used to sketch and draft observations of the angelic body. Today, the paper appeared a face, dark obsidian eyes staring watchfully. Bella Beau was incapable of drawing. Angels are not capable of creating art. For they had never seen enough definition in a human's face to remember or explain into words—they see obscurity, but obscurity in the eyes of the angel is nowhere near the obscurity in the human eyes. Not blurred as frosted glass, an angel could see human's cheery eyes, sweet smiles, and tears of torment. They are all equal. For the angel, a face is a face, a skin surface shielding muscles, bones, and blood. If one is to call it beautiful, then all faces are equally beautiful. A face is not an indication of identity, not the cause for these large wings to halt for a glace...and once looking up from the paper and turning to see the artist—Kwon Cho had found her lighter.

What does it taste like? Bella Beau asked the young lady sitting cross-legged on a wooden chair amidst all the sculptures. Her delicate hand lifted the cigarette to smoke. A long exhale white smoke ensued. Then she shifted her gaze to the angel floating slightly above the floor.

"It's nice. Quite tasty. But it's in here. The taste is in here." The artist's index finger pressed hard against her temples. She inhaled and exhaled the smoke once more. *Like that green candy?* The angel referred to the pill, Kwon Cho knew, and she nodded with a wry smile.

"Yes...just like the candy you mentioned, Bella Beau."

****

If it is human time, ten years must have passed, but I still remember ***the burning heat*** on my fingertips as if it was yesterday...

"Beau! Omma said roasted sweet potatoes are really hot. You can't hold it like that." The small pair of hands grabbed my hand to let the hot sweet potatoes fall to the grass. Kwon Cho was too small to reach up to my face, so she allowed my fingertips to touch her tiny earlobes instead. *Do this, and it will cool down* (something Omma also mentioned), she said. But I didn't feel the heat; how could it cool down? For a moment, the tiny human grabbed my palms that were much bigger than hers and inspected closely. "They will soon turn red." No, they won't. How could it be? I thought to argue...but then my fingertips turned into the color of a pinkish hue; a strange sensation coursed through my skin like never before. *At that time*, I realized that I *unintentionally gave consent* to feel the heat of the half-moon-shaped sweet potato.

After many encounters, this instance that we met during the winter in Seoul was short. On the pavement that the snow fell, throughout our walk, Kwon Cho talked about her Final Project (she called it that, it was probably like her sketchbook since childhood) that had my shadow as a model. She pointed for me to look down. The shadow of a stretched-out winged figure fluttered by the light of tall pillars on the side of the walkway. Suddenly, she asked me to stop walking before taking out her wool scarf. "Let me wrap it up, so you can stay warm." She said she was already warm in her thick sweater and coat. "Come here..." That was another instance I consented...*I consented to the cold wind. For the want to feel the warmth that alleviated the cold. And so I knew...that Kwon Cho's cream color scarf was the warmth amidst the cold that I consented to.*

And so I knew...that the genuine concern from a human was equally warm.

****

"If I don't come back up in two minutes, can you pull me up?"

When you do this, can you breathe?

"I can't...but I might unintentionally fall asleep."

Fall asleep even when you can't breathe? Because of the strangeness of it all, Bella Beau's brows were raised. But Kwon Cho nodded in confirmation.

"Yes..."

Fine, I will pull you back up in two minutes, but tell me, Kwon Cho, *why are you suffocating yourself? For humans, isn't breathing vital?* The angel asked the young woman, naked, submerged inside a bathtub filled with warm water. The black wings swept the floor, but not a single feather had gotten wet amidst the steam that rose like mist. *Humans are strange*, just like Tin Tin said—Bella Beau thought without uttering a word.

"I don't know. You just need to pull me back up." She looked up and lightly touched on the back of the angel's hand. "Promise?" The obsidian eyes stared; a brief silence ensued with the impassive unpredictable expression. And the absolute immaculate face nodded.

"Very well...I promise."

Once answered, the human sank under the water's surface. The steaming warm water overflew from the edge of the tub, and the first second started ticking at that moment. The screams of excruciating pain pierced through the angel's soul. *One more minute...sorrow permeated its ugly smell once more. Another thirty seconds...loneliness spread its dark, ominous shadow. Five. Four. Three. Two. One...*

Kwon Cho.

The angel bowed down to call her name before reaching

both arms to clasp and pull the young woman back from the airless respite as promised. And in her nakedness, Kwon Cho grasped for the embrace from the winged figure with her scarred arms and hands. The scars from the works of her creation. She held Bella Beau tight with all sentimentalities of a ship aimlessly lost at sea, losing a way back to shore. Taking a deep breath, her whole body shook violently with sobs. *Sounds of her cries, loud from her lips, echoed throughout the bathroom chamber, while the screeching scream inside was quieter. Yes...in an instance, it was fading...as if it seemed to almost disappear.*

Without any consolation, only a hand that patted lightly on the young woman's back. Standing still for an embrace, *the angel consented and soaked all over...*

Chapter 5

So, Eternity is the Angel's Fear

"You know...I keep thinking if this is my last sculpture." With unexplained sadness shown on her face, Kwon Cho said those words to the angel who was bathing the moonlight shone through an open window. She smirked, swallowed a green pill along with some form of feelings before closing her eyes, frowned and sighed, smirked once more, and the hammering noise on a chisel began and overcame all sounds.

****

I once asked Tin Tin; *Is there a philosopher among cats?* He wiggled his ears, stretched lazily, and yawned, showing his blunt fangs that looked like the tip of Kwon Cho's colored pencils. He answered; *it is I, the philosopher.* I continued my questioning with much curiosity. What must a cat philosopher know? Must one's wisdom be comprehensive and profound; must one be universally and widely accepted as human philosophers defined?

Why must one do so? No...how could one be so? Widely accepted and universal? It is impossible. Tin Tin's voice sounded like grating a bark, and then he let out a soft sigh. *What I found as the truth might not always be true for other orange cats outside Jeju Island, or even the garden next to this one, their eyes might see differently of a peach—there is no universal Truth for everything, angel...or there is one for humans, I don't know. I know of them less than a drop of water compared to a whole pond.*

I know...just what is true for me, just within my territory, I am my philosopher...

I did not think to argue. Still, I was not so open-minded to concede. Until one day, Tin Tin mentioned a concept I had never had any interest in defining...he talked about ***'an eternity.'***

An eternity. This word creates both a tantalizing promise and a tormenting curse, angel. It is both a true friend and an enemy, both a fresh fish and rotting lettuce. It is...almost everything. I have my own eternity, and Kwon Cho has hers. But sometimes, one feels sympathetic. Because my eternity is ephemeral once compared to Kwon Cho's. This brief eternity hurts her—it hurts her and other humans that give their love to a cat like me. My mother had orange fur, my sister had three colors, the cat at the wooden shed had a roan color. But whatever color they have, all their eternities are brief.

I appreciated this sage from Tin Tin, and I witnessed the cleverness under his round face with long whiskers and orange fur.

And has humans' eternity ever hurt you, black-winged angel?

This was interesting and worth contemplating. I intended to answer him the next time we meet, but alas...Tin Tin's eternity ended. And because of the abrupt ending, in this unexpected void without the orange cat, I had learned the value of briefness in the ethos called 'Eternity.'

****

Deep down, Kwon Cho was immensely curious about the Black-Winged Angel sculpture—whether she is capable of finishing it...or the said marble shall be like all other incomplete works of art, lining up near the walls and paintings, leading to David, the only one standing at the end of the hall.

In Galleria dell' Accademia, on the floor polished to gleam, Bella Beau with their large wings was floating behind Kwon Cho. The artist was walking slowly in her faded sneakers; her mind wandered. As the gaze of her dark eyes traveled through all the sculptures—muscular, immaculate torsos, strong chest muscles, well-defined abdominal muscles according to the conventions of the era, costal grooves, and side ribs were satisfactory, but the limbs and especially the head was still buried in the marble, waiting for the day to be hammered and chiseled into detail—the day that never arrives.

Kwon Cho stopped her steps and stood staring at The Atlas.

Maybe her angelic sculpture will be like this...no, *it must be like this*. If it is to be incomplete, then I hope to communicate clearly beyond the word 'complete' just like this.

Both legs were still drowning in marble; Atlas carried the stone platform that was supposed to be his head. The thick muscular shoulders carried the weight created by the artist...with his face concealed. Still, we can still see the excruciating pressure and the willpower to stand up to fight. Without hearing a word of explanation from Michelangelo's lips, this incomplete but perfect sculpture was named *the Atlas*, the mythical titan who carried heaven on his shoulders. And how heavy the weight of heaven is, we all know.

"Hey...Bella Beau." Because there were tourists of many nationalities in the hall, many different languages compounded together into incomprehensible sounds surrounding Kwon Cho. But with the language she spoke, only the angel could understand or hear. "Have you ever seen a faceless yet beautiful sculpture?" Bella Beau thought for a moment and replied with curiosity. *Similar to humans?* Kwon Cho raised an eyebrow. Her eyes, a small pen-marked mole visible below, glanced at the shadow behind. "What do you mean?"

If it is facial beauty, I could not differentiate, but if you ask about the beauty beyond that...I have seen and still see it always, of course, not with my eyes.

"Do you admire humans?" Because her eyes saw unparalleled perfection floating before her; all hidden within the utmost admirable figure decorated with the miraculous broad raven black wings, the glittering eyes the color of the moonless night, and the melodiously pleasing sound of a meaningful song. All surpassed perfection that a mere human could not imagine a compliment from the angel's lips.

"Bella Beau...the angel that admires humans?"

Yes...I admire the truth that I can sense.

"And are you infatuated by those truths?" Kwon Cho continued walking. She looked past the passersby into the distance at the end of the hall. Like always...she saw David standing majestically on the high stand. The soft surface of white marble radiated brightly with the lamplight. She listened attentively to an answer as loud as a whisper.

One might call it that, but it might not be close. How long can humans stay infatuated?

Because she didn't know, Kwon Cho had no answer.

Is it as long as the days and nights the angel who is infatuated by moonlight travel to the Moon?

"Bella Beau...that is human's whole life." And Kwon Cho thought to herself that *for her, infatuation does not take that long.*

The angel nodded before giving a short answer.

Yes...a lifetime, an eternity, a gift I will give.

Bella Beau's eternity. That revered the heart that sees no horizon of the sky. That remembered all the praises for those wings in perpetuation, despite them not being white. That shall be grateful for the warm tenderness that once felt. And honored art whose value cannot be appraised. At that moment, Kwon Cho's eyes were studying David's face, torso, sex, and feet, without knowing the angel's answer on the matter of eternity—***Bella Beau gave it all for a human—that was her.***

****

The evening at the Piazza, under the gloomy sky that was not completely dark nor the stars could shine. *Why don't you have a cat?* Bella Beau asked because Kwon Cho was sitting on a slowly moving carousel that was spinning round and round. She answered, 'Sometimes, I am lonely...lonely, but I don't need anyone. I don't have a place for them.'

Maybe there was some room at the studio if she removed all the sculptures. She could set up a dining table and build a bigger kitchen. She could probably take out some paintings off the wall to instead install photographs and place a hanger for her coat and bags. But the way of life for Kwon Cho was occupied by art and a strange mood that was completely restrictive. She thought that even standing alone, sometimes she still felt so uncomfortable that she could barely breathe. "Cats should have their place here, too." Bella Beau nodded while starting to enjoy the amusement of a machine that brings one moving up and down similar fluttering wings. "Actually, I used to have a cat...he had orange fur. His name was Tin Tin." This, the angel already knew. "I wish cats could live as long as humans...hey, Bella Beau."

Yes?

"From all the humans you know...when they died, will they see you again?"

Bella Beau's head shook in refusal. The angel waited for the sounds of children shouting and teasing to subside before answering. *I can't tell you about that. It is not a secret...but even me, I'm not sure.*

Kwon Cho pursed her lips. She was disappointed but didn't want to persist and change the question. "You have lived for a long time. You must have faced many losses."

No...not that often. Only a handful of humans could see me. And even fewer when they've grown. Once I'm forgotten and can't be sensed, it is as if I've died from them.

"That sounds more depressing."

If they are friends, sometimes it is...but if they are only passersby, they are only too estranged for me to feel sad.

"And me? Am I your friend, Bella Beau?"

She was about to ask about death. The angel now understood that Kwon Cho and Tin Tin shared a similarity here. If one can breathe, the angel may take a long sigh before answering with a soft voice.

That you are curious, of course, I will be desolate. And even if it is natural, I will be in anguish...naturally.

This answer reminded the human, who was moving up and down riding the carousel horse, about back in the day, her orange cat fell asleep and never woke up again...naturally. The anguish felt natural, and the acceptance of the situation was natural, just like what Bella Beau said.

"I'm sorry" was a dry apology mixed in with a chuckle. Kwon Cho looked up at the sky above the round-roof building decorated with bright orange lightbulbs. A long inhalation, piercing cold air hurt her nose. She felt cold. The feeling flooded through her chest. She thought that the smell of old books and vanilla candles was so fitting for the angel. "I'm sorry...that I don't live that long, Bella Beau."

A lifespan, who can choose? Why do you have to apologize? Besides, a limited lifetime has an immeasurable benefit. As the carousel passed by, Bella Beau turned to a painter selling paintings next to the nearby bench. In the last two rounds, he had just squeezed a paint into a wooden plate, but now he had already started spreading the paint onto paper with a brush as big as a feather. ***Kwon Cho, do you know why angels don't paint or build a sculpture?***

"..."

But if my life is shorter...perhaps, angels might start picking a hammer and chisel to build something eternal. ***Perhaps, there might have been a David with broad wings spreading wide at his back.***

****

People called this place a *nightclub*...

This place where the light was dim as the dawn, the music was playing as humans nodded their heads to a slow rhythm, like a flock of birds on a branch. Strangely flavored beverages lined up...a cherry in a glass; it tasted completely different from a cherry from a garden.

Kwon Cho said she was drunk. And I thought that being drunk was a perplexing symptom. It wasn't easy for me to comprehend what the Human spoke of. Because she kept talking about philosophy, the teachings of Socrates, the curious case of Las Meninas, and suddenly changed the topic to the art of flower arrangement by geisha. "I wish I could arrange the flowers that beautifully. I'll put together the magnolias with orange blossoms and sunflowers. After that, I will brew and sip Gyokuro tea."

I had difficulty finding a connection of it all...thus, being drunk was perplexing. But it was a symptom that revealed and stripped bare stories of the heart. The sound from one's lips perfectly resonated stories in one's head.

She wanted to talk, wanted to be, wanted to arrange, wanted to drink, wanted to smell, or even...

"I want to kiss you...angel." Kwon Cho said before her hot lips were pressed against the back of my hand. To that, she said she wanted to know what angels smell like. 'Like a book, like a vanilla pod...no, like a vanilla candle.' I did not deny it. Because like my facial features, she perceived what she desired. As for the kiss she requested, I didn't reject it. Because a kiss had no more inherent meaning to me than simply looking into each other's eyes, talking, or a naive touch of a fingertip on a palm.

In an alley away from the nightclub, beneath the big tree, the flowers began to bloom; altogether, they were like white dots. Kwon Cho kissed me. Her face was close but could not be seen clearly even once I observed more carefully...thus, I closed my eyes. I felt her palm on the back of my neck, another palm caressing my cheek, her breath smelled of cherry wine, and her warm moist lips from a kiss bestowed without any feeling between us...and once broke away, Kwon Cho frowned.

"Hey...was it that bad?" At first, I thought this was from an awkward lack of confidence. "It's rude to make that face after a kiss, don't you know, angel?" But I wasn't quite right. I thought again that Kwon Cho was livid—this word was more accurate. Nonetheless, I lifted the corners of my lips to smile, widened my eyes, and told her that *it wasn't bad, but I just felt unaffected.* With this answer, Kwon Cho forced a peculiar laugh.

"Unaffected?"

Yes, it is normal...I felt good, but 'good' is the same feeling as us standing here talking.

"And sex? Do you also feel unaffected?"

I knew the meaning of sex that the human meant. I had experienced this on some occasions. But at the same time...

Yes, sex is identical to listening to you talking about Epicurus and the inscription on his tomb. Once I finished, Kwon Cho's smile widened until I saw her white teeth. As she moved closer, I instinctively spread my wings.

"I felt the same." She said so. And we kept walking together in a narrow alley. Loud was the sound of loneliness from people in high-rise buildings from a distance.

"Anyways, do you have a name, angel?"

Yes...I do. My name is Bella Beau.

"Wow, beautiful name. I like your name, Bella Beau."

****

Because she was barefoot while working and wasn't cautious enough, once the chisel drilled into the marble piece destined to be shaped into a wing, a sharp marble fragment fell and landed on her feet. The nail-like edge punctured and left a wound. Without any cuss or cry, Kwon Cho frowned, looking down at the blood seeping from her skin. "Too bad..." The young woman put down things in her hand. She walked over to widen the window, only had a brief glance at the Moon, and went back to light a cigarette as if it had the power to alleviate pain. "Beau...please take a rest. I need to do something about it first." She spoke of the ruby-red blood all over the back of her feet. The wound was bigger than expected, and the bleeding was more severe than she initially assumed. Still, she leaned against the window frame, dropping her weight on one leg. Her face was wry while inhaling the smoke. "It hurts when seeing a lot of blood." To that end, she took a sharp inhale and breathed out white smoke. Once she saw that Bella Beau walked closer, Kwon Cho turned her face away before squishing a cigarette butt on the same old cracked saucer.

Hurry. Treat your wound.

The angel warned and handed her a small box as if knowing that the artist who always gets injured from her work was in need of it. But once seeing that the young woman still had no response, their eyes locked in a brief moment, her tired eyes broke away, and she looked at the sculpture in the middle of the room instead. Hence, the winged figure had to kneel, the widespread black wings swiftly folded behind the back, the angel bent down, the tip of Beau's nose almost touched the back of her wounded foot. At that moment... Kwon Cho withdrew her foot before hurriedly bending down to grab the box and sat quietly on the sofa. Finally, she got to patch up her wound. But even so, the angel followed and sat on the floor beside her to observe drops of blood being cleaned out by a cotton ball.

In that serene silence, the angel thought of all the drops of blood one had seen, from blood seeping through a knee scrape wound to a large pool of blood streamed from a civil war. When the angel's conscious mind returned from memories, the wound at the back of Kwon Cho's foot was already treated. *Is everything being taken care of?*

"Yes, that's all there is."

Will you really be okay?

"Yes, of course...yes."

Is it true?

"Yeah..." Because she was asked three times, Kwon Cho started to knit her brows, and her dark eyes narrowed and stared at the angel. Not because she was frustrated but because she was curious about what was on the angel's mind. Kwon Cho extended her hand to touch Bella Beau's shoulder. The angel still had preoccupying worry about the health of her right foot. The beautiful face leaned on the sofa cushion, staring at the bandaged wound so close that the young lady thought it strange. "Is something wrong?" She asked in a hushed voice once both of their eyes met.

If you bleed again, you need to treat your wound. Please...

"..."

Or if you don't want to do it, just ask me; I will unquestionably handle the task... but you must tell me, Kwon Cho.

If she was not mistaken...Kwon Cho thought that this was the angel's fear.

"Um, I get it." She then knew—like humans' fright, ***angels can be consumed by fear all the same.***

Chapter 6

In the Arms of an Angel

"Minju said the drawing Kwon Cho did was wrong. It was really wrong." Kwon Cho talked about the paper lying on the grass near her school bag. As for her, she was holding my wings, splaying them apart and folding them back, and splaying the wings again to neatly place flowers between the feathers. *What color should it be?* She mumbled as I eyed that paper once more before holding it up to examine. Another reimagination of my image that Kwon Cho painted with watercolors that were predominantly *black*. "An angel must have white wings. Minju told me that."

Is that so? And what do you think? I asked Kwon Cho, who was busy embroidering white grass flowers in between my black feathers. Tiny human tiptoed enthusiastically to reach beyond her height. So, I lowered my wings without her asking. Just to stay closer.

"She just doesn't know." A tiny hand handed me a grass flower with a color unlike others. I graciously received it and smelled its soft scent. *Grass flowers and their banality in smell. But this banality creates the smell of a season.* "Minju just doesn't know that an angel can have wings in many colors like flowers. If she knows, she must like them. Because Minju loves flowers the most."

****

"Damn it..." was a short cuss uttered before a loud noise exploded as if lightning struck in the middle of the high-ceiling studio. A soft white beam of light emanated through the window; it gleamed like theater lamps. The oil painting on canvas was violently thrashed against the floor. The artist hoisted it above her head, raised her arms high, and thrashed the object again with great force. Again and again, until the wooden frame was wrecked into bits. Paints peeled off, and the canvas was torn. The dirt and debris flew through the air. She was panting, a slow but firm rhythm. And for the angel who felt the deep hidden emotion in her soul. *The wave of anger had just passed, but the insidious disappointment polluted with foul cynicism was forming into a new surge.*

"Who does she think she is to dare criticize my work? ***Kwon Cho's work is just a meaningless mystery. Color shades seem to have stories to tell, but in truth, they are***

simply an empty abyss. Ugh! Who the hell cares?"

She seemed to ignore the hurtful criticism, but the reality was quite the opposite. Otherwise, the precious paintings, in Bella Beau's opinion, might not get taken down from the wall and piled on the ground indignantly like this. "How could she dare say that? How good are her paintings? How profound are they?"

Since those were essentially statements and not questions, the angel remained silent.

"That woman...the audacity!"

****

Kwon Cho...and what if Minju doesn't like it? If your friends and other people don't like it, will you still like this painting? Once she heard the question, Kwon Cho and her small bouquet of grass flowers stood still for a second. She frowned in contemplation. Her small eyes stared at her painting—*The Angel with Black Wings*, the painting in my hand.

I'm just waiting for the answer...the answer that I can only hope that in the future, Kwon Cho will give the same answer always.

"I will like it. Kwon Cho...I have to like my own work, of course. My paintings are so awesome! Even an angel complimented me. My works are the best!"

I wish with all my being for this answer to last throughout Kwon Cho's eternity...

****

In front of the sculpture, the hammering noise stopped temporarily when a question emerged in her mind.

"Bella Beau...do angels have magic?" The young artist could not remember, but this was the second time she asked about the angel's magical power.

Yes...but in my view, the magic you mentioned is a trade.

"A trade?"

Yes...a trade.

"How? With money?"

We trade two things with equal worth. As for human money, it is of no use.

"Really? It's useless to you, just numbers, worthless pieces of paper. Is that so?"

Not quite. Money is not worthless. Money is given worth. Hence it has value. But I don't estimate the worth of things with a prejudiced, lax, and rapidly changing scale—like money. A blooming flower costs 10 dollars. A time-traveling trip may cost a hundred dollars. And a life is worth one thousand dollars. The prices may be the same for all buyers, but the values are never identical in the minds of each human being.

We should not trade flower petals for our life treasure.

And we shall not trade our eternity with leftover coins from anyone's pocket.

I don't follow the usual perceived rules. Hence, an angel doesn't trade with money, Kwon Cho.

The young woman thought of valuable treasures in her life. Of course, the first thing that came to mind was her arts. The second was the tools to build those arts. And the third...for a brief moment, she thought of herself. She thought of her skills and expertise she considered to be valuable but then shook her head, let out a sigh, let go of the thought, and continued to hammer on the chisel that pierced into the marble.

Days and nights passed, some slow, some fast, while the beautifully crafted figure progressed closer to perfection as anticipated. Its broad wings were carved to sway with feathers. The face on the marble was left blank; only a structure was apparent—which was a subject of much concern for Kwon Cho. She was standing on a step ladder, staring so close she almost touched the face of the angel with her face. Her dark eyes gaze all over, finding details she might have missed. But none escaped her eyes. All that was visible, Kwon Cho was certain that nothing escaped her eyes. It was a curious case that the immaculate beauty could not be replicated with a hammer and chisel. It was a curious case that no matter how bright and white the fine stone can be, the glimmers resonated from it were unparalleled to the words and songs of the angel. *It was a matter of great curiosity and at the same time...unfortunate.*

She could smell old papers. Her fingertips touched the angel's cheekbone and moved to the tip of the chin—all were indifferent from her own skin.

Perhaps, you can see better? Because we were so close, when the angel bowed slightly, the forehead had touched the human's warm temple. Kwon Cho laughed. She let out a soft smile and voiced out a protest because it was too close. Too close that everything was just a blur. "I think it is only you...that can hear and see everything clearly." *Maybe you have to close your eyes.* The young woman did not expect to see anything in that darkness Bella Beau had invited. But she complied. Kwon Cho closed her eyes.

Oh...no...God. She cried out inside.

Do you have more clarity?

"..." Yes, But the clarity was not the angelic perfection. In the darkness, a soft lullaby seemed to whisper and console. Kwon Cho saw the trace of her own emotions that left a large ugly cut in her mind. The cut was deep. Its silence surrendered without explanation. *This wound is this deep and hideous? Since when...*

Do you see it clearly, Kwon Cho?

"Yes..." She uttered an answer. Her sad face tinted with a faint smile nodded as she opened her eyes.

Is there anything I can do to help, Kwon Cho?

She shook her head. Confusion was shown in her eyes. She looked down, the brows furrowed in a deep crease. After the angel repeated the question, she shook her head once again.

"No, nothing."

If that is so, can I hug you, Kwon Cho?

****

In an embrace of the angel that held her with both arms and black wings, Kwon Cho thought that this narrow space cordially invited her to lie on her back more than a soft grass field ever could. It incited her thoughts to drift away more so than the seashore. It offered more tranquility for her mind than a pine forest. *Bella Beau's embrace...was spacious; it was full of light and contentment.*

And on the pavement in the evening that rain fell, suddenly, the young artist sobbed. Amidst the falling raindrops, the passerby might have seen her crying and getting soaked in absolute loneliness. But in truth, Kwon Cho wasn't quite alone. Because the tearful face sobbed on the shoulders of the angel, invisible from others' sight, while the wide wings shielded her from the cruel cold wind and rain.

I'm miserably depressed...and damaged without a way out, Bella Beau.

I know...Kwon Cho. I know that well.

Chapter 7

Goodbye, My Angel

I ***hear a bird sings and smell the sweet fragrance of flowers.*** The weather this morning was bright. I observed Kwon Cho. She was using iron filings to shape my marble wings. Her fingertips caressed the surface, considering its smoothness; when it was still rough to the touch, she continued to polish it attentively. *It was unsettling*. Humans must call it that, this feeling. I thought she would not be able to see me the next day. Lost in the ability to hear my voice or perceive my existence. *Not for long. For her, there will be no black-winged angel.*

Other than flocks of birds and a field of flowers...when I looked up, I saw the dawn of farewell. The morning sun emerged over the horizon and shone its ray of light bright over Kwon Cho.

****

"How much is my work worth, angel? If I can trade all this stuff, what can I get in exchange?"

I followed to the end of her hand, gesturing to the sculptures and paintings. *Almost everything...that I would be willing to trade.* Kwon Cho smiled...a strange smile. *No...it wasn't a smile.*

"Can I trade death in exchange?"

I was astounded. If I had a heart—it would break.

"If I ask for death...will you give me that?"

Why do you ask for such a thing?

"Because I have nothing left to ask..." Her still wounded hand let go of the hammer; it fell to the floor near the chisel. Kwon Cho moved away from the sculpture. She lit a cigarette and expressionlessly gazed out the window. *"The same as that in Socrates' hemlock, that in Sophonisba's cup, that in Juliet's kiss...do you have some of that, Bella Beau?"*

Yes...I do. But you cannot trade all your arts with it. For arts are immortal; even when the artists die, the arts survive.

"Then, what can I give you in exchange?"

If I bestow to you your demise, in vice-versa, you shall likewise bestow it to be mine. Death shall be upon me all the same. Not with my body. But my soul will perish for all eternity.

My existence will forever be overcome by darkness for all eternity.

****

"Bella Beau."

What is it...what is it, Kwon Cho? If she could understand the language of cats, I assumed Kwon Cho must have talked to Tin Tin all day because Kwon Cho was always full of questions, queries that if it was Tin Tin, he might have answered them better than I ever did.

"Do you know death?"

I have some knowledge of it. But why do you ask?

"Well, Aunty Kim just passed away. Omma said we all have to die all the same...but for Kwon Cho, for me, I don't want to die." I nodded, seeing it as natural for humans; they do not know death at first, but once acknowledged, hearing tales of unavoidable and irreversibly certainty, most tiny humans do not want to face death, both for themselves, their family, their pet, or even their favorite toy. "If I die, then I can't draw, right?" Kwon Cho pouted her lips to sulk. A Tutti Frutti box was opened, and the sweets got poured out for the green pieces to be separated. She held the box tightly in her hand. *"Kwon Cho wants to draw every day..."*

I am uncertain whether there are papers, pencils, and paint drops in the human afterlife. ***But today in life, there are****. If it is me, today I will draw anything I desire.*

"Is it so? Is there enough time? Kwon Cho wants to draw thousands and millions and millions of pictures."

Once small, one was full of dreams, but once grown, some humans call for death as if demise is a retreat in the midst of summer as if the cemetery is the seashore, and a tombstone is a rock in the middle of the calm sea. Perhaps the storm of hardships one must face days after days narrows their options into seeking a vacation that life fails to offer...humans deserve sympathy—no matter they are tiny humans who seek to avoid death or grown ones that demand it. All are sympathetic. An angel can grant a blessing; some humans believe that. If I can grant a blessing, I shall wish all human a weekend holiday from excruciating suffering and deep void of desolation. For they shall not ask God for death, from others, or even oneself. For they shall see great seas antithetical to graveyards. For they shall rally in a tranquil forest instead of a lonesome cemetery... **I shall grant that blessing.**

You might not draw thousands and millions and millions of pictures at once, but perhaps, if you draw every day, there will be countless pictures. That is what I think.

And Kwon Cho nodded before she deposited a Tutti Frutti into my hand. She rushed to pick up a color box and papers and declared to draw every day from now on...

I smiled and looked at a small heap of green Tutti Fruttis in my palm.

****

In the darkness of night tonight, the immaculate figure of the angel was invisible.

The opaque pill bottle was emptied just like a Tutti

Frutti box—all green pills poured into the hand that recently ditched a cigarette butt.

"..."

Kwon Cho. The angel called. But there was no reply. No gestures or facial expressions indicated she heard any call. The first pill was put in her mouth and swallowed. Her bare feet stepped around the dusty floor of the room. She bent down to pick a vinyl record of a sharp violin piece and played. Three more pills were swallowed. And she raised her arms high to dance with herself and the Moon. The music from the phonograph horn was her company.

As if the young woman could no longer hear the pleas from the angel. And the winged figure's hand reached out to touch her arm but passed her like air, like the soft wind, too soft for her senses.

Kwon Cho...

****

The artist who adored her work beyond anything placed a kiss on the marble angel's face. She bid farewell. A caress on the beautiful wings one last time before stepping down from the wooden stand...Kwon Cho circled around the studio. In her thunderstorm of emotions, this place was a sorrowful cemetery and a precious museum. So, she drowned in its pleasing comfort and a solemn curse; both smiled and sobbed.

Fingertips caressed past all lined up sculptures. For a moment, her worn-out and swollen eyes stared at Apollo's face. *There will be no more sunrise at dawn.* Her parch lips moved to a grin, and she laughed before forcing all pills held in her hand down her throat; some swallowed, some fell and scattered like green stars on the mottled floor. Some rolled around and rested at the feet of the invisible angel. Kwon Cho hummed a melody following the sound of a violin. Her body swayed with her arms spread out like wings—she spun around, lost it all midair, and fell...

All her limbs paralyzed, and breathing slowed...

In a split second...only a fragment of time, the briefness of moment when a butterfly fluttered its wings that she thought...

I want to live...more than anything.

****

Because in that split second, she asked for her life, the split second was more than enough. In that astoundingly brief instant, I embraced her body that was a mere shell for a nearly perished soul in my arms. In that briefness of time, I came to be once more, I regained my voice, I revived my senses...Kwon Cho accepted my plea.

And I graciously welcomed it.

Now, I heard the shattering sound of the soul...

I greeted death when the black feathers floated in the air like a flock of birds flying through the sky. On the floor of the human lying unconscious on my body, I extended my disappearing hand to touch her closed eyelids.

I grant you my eternity. For you to live as long as I could live in memories of a human. As for the eternity you had offered, I shall return to accept. Someday.

****

When she woke up the next morning, the pill bottle and the cigarette pack became garbage that needed to be disposed of. Kwon Cho walked to the incomplete sculpture. The sunlight shone on her soft white skin. She touched a finger to her lips. She tried to recall the memory of what she intended to create.

She was surprised she recalled nothing...

She couldn't recall even slightly on features she intended to carve on the face of this sculpture. That angel, with that beautiful self, what do that immaculate facial features look like? Where had the perfection that lay deep beneath flown to? A bright blue sky...will the black-winged figure return? Strange questions swirling in her head. ***Decisively, she engraved it—the black wings tattoo deep in her skin.***

Once the sky is bright blue...

Perhaps, I will see an angel... Someday.

End Credit

Longa

In the corner of suburban Florence, in a small rental apartment that a resident recently moved in. *Bella Beau* thinks one's initial estimation on the room was inaccurate—all these art pieces need more space; there must be cupboards, hangers, and stands. Otherwise, there wouldn't be any space left to sleep on. Because even with the six-foot-long bed, the area is occupied with a large post box that takes all the space of the dark purple bedsheet.

The sender was *Kwon Cho*...

Bella Beau purses her lips and contemplates. She unbuttons the top shirt button, loosens the necktie, and takes off the coat before placing it near the bed. The sweat from the body forces the tall figure to walk to the window and push it wide open. Eyes closed, feeling the soft wind caressing the skin, she smiles and walks back to pour her attention to the package on the bed.

First thing first, beginning with opening the letter...

The letter from the artist that imaginatively created the sculpture she successfully auctioned. The beautiful marble sculpture is now standing near the bed.

To Miss Bella Beau,

I must admit that you gave me a pleasant surprise. For the paintings I have sent you, too often that most collectors would demand for them and offer a price so high that astonishes me. But I am never willingly to sell it to anyone. I have kept them as if I was waiting for something, or may I correct myself—waiting for someone.

On the day that we walked through the rain together (if you may recall). It might be for no reason at all that I thought of these paintings...for week, I've tried to think of the reasons why but found none. However, although there is no reason for it, I want to gift you these paintings. Please do not offer or ask for the price, because I will not take it.

Because in my head...it is as if all these paintings are yours since the first charcoal mark was drawn from my pencil.

P.S. Next week, I will have an art exhibition at the Uffizi Gallery. If you have time, I hope we can meet again.

Hope to see you later.
Kwon Cho

When the box opens and reveals the object inside, she gently takes out the frame with both hands.

Because for Bella Beau, all these art pieces are precious, long-lasting, and the nearest to the word 'eternity.'

A bright smile brushes across her lips, the glittering obsidian eyes gazed upon the canvas, on the colorful paintbrush strokes, on the painting of *the Angel's Embrace, the Angel's Songs, and the Death of an Angel.*

****

'I grant you my eternity. For you to live as long as I could live in memories of a human. As for the eternity you had offered, I shall return to accept. Someday.'

All these...are the eternity Kwon Cho has given her.

The End

“

To a garden of flowers
vast enough for all diverseness of flowers.

For loneliness to be embraced.
For the relinquished to be chased.

I wish you an orange cat,
Bella Beau,
and a Tutti Frutti in your bag always...

www.ingramcontent.com/pod-product-compliance
Ingram Content Group UK Ltd.
Pitfield, Milton Keynes, MK11 3LW, UK
UKHW041951190726
13854UKWH00005B/1903

9 781915 214669